CHRYSALIS

KIMBERLY REI

For my usagi…

All of it, love

Kim, November 2020

TABLE OF CONTENTS

CHAPTER ONE

The child was pulled screaming from her dead mother's womb. Her cries shattered the moonless, starless night, scaring birds from the trees. Had Chani still been drawing breath, had she been alive for the birth of her daughter, she would have been proud. Instead, her husband's warriors cheered at the storm of good omens. To them, such a child was a gift from the spirits. Born in the secret of the dark, she would carry the strength of her mother, as well as her own and bring great victory to the tribe. They spoke among themselves, pounding each other on the back as if they had something to do with the birth.

Twin wise women looked up, one from the dead woman's belly, the other from the babe. Matching scowls went ignored. The two were only ever consulted when their talents were needed. Had the chief's wife not been so near her time, they would have been left behind. The wife may have died, but that was not uncommon in childbirth. She had done her duty. The girl was all that mattered. A child born of blood and pain and fear. She was destined for greatness. The twins leaned closer, so the brash men wouldn't hear their whispering.

"This mark. Do you see? It is a sign of..."

"...the spirits. This child must..."

"...be protected. We will keep..."

"...her and raise her."

"And teach her."

Midiga met Sidanthe's gaze, their bond now removing all need for words. The warriors would attempt to raise this child in their ways, understanding only death, the sword her only talent. But they saw more. So much more.

Sidanthe didn't protest when Gaven pulled the child from her arms and held the girl aloft. Deep voices raised in a battle cry of welcome and triumph. They laughed as she wailed.

Midiga watched carefully as Sidanthe turned her back on the men and dipped her fingers into the gaping belly, coating her fingers in blood. She listened to the child cry and the men laugh, allowing the noise to cover her chanting as she drew runes in the dirt. Midiga bent forward, eyes never leaving the men, and spat over the runes. The symbols glowed, blood hissing as the spit burned and blazed. Chanting softer, Sidanthe swept her hand over the writing and the ground rippled, runes fading away.

A shift of motion caught Midiga's attention. She looked up into the glittering eyes of Bredin—their chief. His jaw twitched as he looked upon his daughter. The love between Bredin and Chani was legendary. Most bindings were done out of necessity and politics. Tribes gathered twice a year to show off their most beautiful and accomplished young women. Bredin had set eyes on Chani at such a gathering, and ignoring protocol, declared her his wife on the spot. She could have refused—they weren't barbarians, after all—four men stood ready to take Bredin's place at a single word from her. But the word she spoke disappointed them all. She accepted his offer, and that night, her cries of pleasure made half the camp uncomfortable. The other half rose to the occasion. And now she was gone, giving birth to the only child Bredin would sire with her. Tears filled his eyes, and he allowed the twins to see. A moment later, he was once again stern and in control.

"Declare her path, Seers. Where shall she thrive?"

A soundless sigh of relief echoed between the sisters. They had known their chief since his own birth, so many moons ago. Normally level-headed, he had been known to lash out, irrational and angry. There had been a chance, however small, that he would end the child. Or worse, demand to raise her himself.

"She belongs with..."

"...us. She will make..."

"...you proud, Lord."

A single nod and a last look at his beloved wife, "You will name her Iana, as her mother chose." He turned away, dismissing all creatures female. "Prepare to ride!"

Sidanthe gripped the pendant hanging from the dead woman's neck and pulled it free. Her body would remain here, nourishing animal and earth both. The pendant would be given to the child in time.

They struck camp that night at the edge of the woods. The superstitious warriors dared not draw close to the dense forest. Too many tales had been spun of spirits and mythical demons. The wise women shared a secret smile, for they had been the weavers of many of them.

They nodded to Bredin and tucked their cloaks tighter as they stepped onto an ancient, loamy path where they would have privacy.

A short walk brought them to a clearing where the grass glowed softly. They sat before each other, cross-legged, and laid the babe between them. The glow drew in closer, narrowing until only the child rested in its light.

Sidanthe held the pendant over the newborn and watched as it began to spin. Faster and faster, tightening the chain, then drawing upward. Smoke began to rise from the chain. The archaic symbol blazed scarlet. Sidanthe maintained her grip until the heat grew to be too much. She pulled the necklace away from the child and watched as it instantly cooled. She met Midiga's eyes, seeing her own fear mirrored there.

They spoke to each other silently, on a plane of awareness none of their tribe could imagine. They did not finish sentences or speak over one another. Their voices became one and while they conversed, there was no difference between them.

"This will not be an easy child to raise. We must take great care with her and surround her with love. Her mother lingers too close."

CHAPTER TWO

The little girl played in the garden. Sidanthe had made a game of weeding and identifying plants, and now the three-year-old giggled as she ripped weeds out. If she occasionally caught an herb in her enthusiastic fingers, no harm was done. The rare and poisonous were kept safely fenced off. Iana wasn't tall enough to step over the gateless enclosure. Sidanthe smiled and gently guided the child to another section needing her tender ministrations. Movement caught her attention, and she leaned down, pointing. "Look, Iana. A rabbit!"

"Abbit! Abbit!"

Iana pulled, trying to chase after the white fluff ball, but Sidanthe held her back with kindness and laughter. "No no, dearest. Let the rabbit be about his business. As long as he doesn't eat our lunch, he's alright. And speaking of lunch, are you hungry? As soon as we're done here, we'll go eat, shall we?"

"Aw, nuts!"

Iana's favourite expression had been picked up from one of the village boys. She had been delighted that a word she was allowed to say could also be used to swear. She'd tried out a variety of other curses and they had all gotten her scolded. This one seemed to be safe, so she used it often and not without some irony.

The sun was just cresting its highest place when the weeding was quite suddenly done. Sidanthe always loved this task for just that reason. It went from overwhelming and tedious to over, with little in between. She rose and dusted off her dress. "Come, Iana. Lunch! I think we even have some milk left over."

The child raced out of the garden and stopped on the path. She looked up, head tilting curiously. And then she screamed and dropped to the stones, thrashing and howling. Sidanthe ran to her, calling to her sister in a loud, frantic voice, "Midiga! Oh gods, Midiga, come quick!"

In seconds, both twins crouched over the twitching girl. She had calmed physically, but had begun to babble. The sisters exchanged worried looks. Iana was only three and had never been clear of speech. She still had a little girl's lilt and a charming way of mangling words. Sentences were only managed if she was parroting someone. But as she lay on the ground, her small body jerking, she spoke in very clear sentences.

Of bright lights in the sky, far beyond reach, spinning and exploding. Of other places and other beings. Such things were frightening but could be written off as fantasy and creation. It was when she began speaking of the villagers that the twins grew truly concerned.

"She is a seer, of great..."

"...power. Even we could not..."

"...predict the future so..."

"...clearly. She must not..."

Midiga braced herself against the inevitable and placed her hand over Iana's mouth. "Hush, child. You must not speak. You must never speak again." To give voice to the words was to lose their power. The strongest and most sure of seers drew pictures and words on hides that were treasured. Offering prophecy to the wind was a foolish waste. There had not been a Seer of Truth in many generations. As talented as the twins were, they relied on signs and practicality. Of course, the blacksmith's daughter would bear a girl—that was all the family seemed able to create. Yes, the crops would be bountiful this harvest—the rains had come early and strong. Even Iana's birthmark, a small crescent on her ankle, was nothing more than a sign—a sign that the warriors would have taken as evil; had the sisters not claimed her at her birth, she would have been drowned as soon as it was discovered.

But *this*? This was the true gift. One they had only heard of around the women's fire and read in crumbling texts. They knew what to do, though. The child fell silent under Midiga's commanding touch. Sidanthe was the gentler of the two; Iana had learnt swiftly to never cross Midiga. But it was with a great tenderness that Midiga lifted her in strong arms, cradling her close. It was with great grief that she laid the child on the only table in the tiny cabin. If her tears fell on the girl's cheek as Sidanthe held down the twisting body and she sewed tiny lips closed, perhaps she could be forgiven.

CHAPTER THREE

Iana stood over the body of the fox, tears streaming down her cheeks. Her slight frame trembled with distress. Sidanthe watched from across the garden and restrained the urge to run to the child. Death was inevitable in their world and happened often. Human and animal alike were bound to the whim of the spirits. One must show the spirits strength that they might find you worthy of life. To comfort another over death was to imply the spirits had made a mistake and that would hasten one's own exit. Sidanthe kept her hands busy but continued to watch Iana with a careful eye. She saw the child kneel down and touch the fox. She saw the red fur ripple as if something moved just under the surface. And as she stood and called out to Midiga, she watched the girl's body go perfectly still and the fox leap to its feet. She held up a hand as Midiga, annoyance bristling, came from the shed.

The fox shook itself. At first, the head lolled to the side, neck still broken from the fall that killed it. And then it straightened. Cracked left. Cracked right. And turned to look at the twins. Human eyes blinked and the fox took an unsteady step forward. Panic and hesitation warred. It took another step and another. Finally, the fox ran straight to Sidanthe and huddled against her legs. She met Midiga's look and sighed.

"A gift from her mother. A dual..."

"...talent. Control over death..."

"...and bodywalking. Dangerous..."

"...to all of us. We must teach..."

"...and protect her, yes. We will announce..."

"...her place in the village. I will consult the scrolls."

Sidanthe reached down and rubbed the fox's head. "Very good, child. Do you think you can step back into yourself now? Go try. You cannot stay a fox for always. A fox won't help in the garden!"

She laughed and nudged the small body, hiding her fear. The creature ran back to the kneeling girl and as soon as it nuzzled the limp hand, the body dropped to the ground, dead once more. Iana stood and dusted off her knees. She stared at the fox thoughtfully. As she turned to the sisters, Sidanthe touched Midiga's arm, stilling the instinctive retreat from an all too ancient gaze. A moment later, the child was back, racing to the garden to pull weeds.

***

On the next full moon, the twins took Iana to the village square. Some of the tribe had not seen the girl since she was a babe and were shocked by the sewn lips. Questions fluttered, passed in whispers. The sisters ignored all and walked Iana to the chief. He raised himself a little taller but showed no other response to his daughter. His new wife looked on the child with disdain and rubbed her belly. She would give birth any day and saw Iana as a mere irritation.

As the crowd gathered around the square, the chief nodded to Midiga. She stepped up onto the stone platform and pulled Iana with her.

"My people, hear my words! You have a new seer among you! Born in darkness and tragedy, she is destined to lead you to greatness. It has been generations since one of such power has walked among us and so you may find her strange. But do not fear and do not dismay, for the spirits have made themselves known through her. Her gift is true! Please, step forward and meet Iana, Seer of the Atar!"

Whispers spread through those gathered, voices quiet with awe and wonder. They pressed forward as Midiga pulled Iana onto the platform. Some reached out as if to touch her. One woman held her child back with a protective arm. Iana huddled against Midiga. She had been to the village before, but never under such scrutiny. And not at all since her voice had been silenced. Sidanthe stepped up as well, crowding the stone. She smiled and raised both hands, quieting the growing chatter.

"I know many of you have questions for Iana, but we do not wish to wear her out. We will return at the new moon, ready to hear you and respond."

CHAPTER FOUR

Every villager turned out on the day of their return, each with a question. When the twins arrived with Iana, they almost turned back; such a crowd was surely intimidating. But Iana let go of both their hands and moved to sit at the table in the middle of the square.

She smiled gently to the first person to step up, a woman heavy with child. This was young Fayne, who had lost two children already. One was stillborn, the other had died before her second year. Fayne's husband had threatened to set her out if she didn't provide an heir. He was no treasure, but he provided a home and demanded little but a warm bed. Divorce was no shame in the village. Many of those gathered had been wed more than once. Indeed, spouses were sometimes traded, and the new matches were much happier. But to be known as one who cannot breed or care for a child was a mark no woman could bear. Errinaya, the tribal witch, lived at the outer edges of tribal lands, visited only when a potion or spell was needed. It was her only option after failing to rise with child across two marriages. The spirits clearly did not find her worthy of motherhood. It was said, though, that they did gift her with other skills and men were often seen leaving her cabin.

The sisters couldn't hear what was asked, but as they watched, Iana reached out and touched Fayne. She made a motion and Fayne blushed, but lifted her shirt enough to let Iana's small hand slip under. There was a tense moment as Iana's eyes closed. It seemed even the birds stopped singing. Midiga made a mental note. That happened a lot around the child. But then Iana looked up into Fayne's eyes and a smile threatened to tear the stitches from her lips. Fayne's hands flew to her mouth to still a cry of hope. Iana nodded and tugged the woman's shirt back into place, patting the belly with affection. She made a motion of sound coming from her own lips, then pointed to herself.

As the sisters moved closer, they could hear Fayne reply, joy laced in every word. "Oh yes! I will name her... her? It's a girl? Yes! I will name her for you, Seer. Oh, thank you!"

With tears flowing, Fayne ran to her mother's

arms. Both left, babbling with plans and happiness.

And so the day went. The twins ensured that Iana stopped to eat and rest, but the child insisted on staying until every question was answered. For the most part, she could answer in hand motions and elaborate expressions. A quill and stack of parchment was close at hand for the more complex. One argument broke out when Dask asked about planting barley in the east field. Iana shook her head and tried to tell him tubers would be better. Dask hated tubers. He pretended to not understand her and made her respond to every other possible crop until she grabbed a sheet of parchment and scrawled: "Tubers, you a—" Sidanthe had yanked the quill out of small fingers and murmured something about the child needing a break.

Some left in tears and some left with a great deal to think about. It was not in a Seer to lie or honey-coat a truth. Most, though, left with either a smile or an eased heart. Even Bredin's new wife, Gwethana, asked after her impending birth. She was disturbed by the promise of a deep struggle, but relieved that the boy would be born healthy. She was also puzzled that Iana treated her like everyone else until Sidanthe gently pointed out that Iana had no idea Bredin was her father. She knew him as the chief, nothing more. Sidanthe's only comment to Midiga was that perhaps Gwethana would be kinder to their ward in the future.

The last villager left as the sun started its journey to the nightlands. Iana swayed on her feet and Midiga moved to lift her. A quiet, sad voice spoke behind them.

"I have my cart here. I would be honoured to help take the young Seer home."

Midiga turned to face Cydare. She took in the slump of shoulders and the tired grief in his eyes. He had asked Iana about a pain in his belly that would not go away. Learning he wouldn't live to see the harvest was hard. But he had thanked her for honesty and warning. It gave him, he said, time to settle his family and his herd.

"As you sure, shepherd? The day has been long for all."

He smiled, and Sidanthe was struck by his youth. His tale would be a tragedy in the village. He nodded and stepped aside, drawing his hand cart closer. It was small, meant to be taken to and from the market. But it was more than enough for Iana and was already padded with bags of wool for sale.

"Please. Allow me to thank her for treating me kindly and granting me the gift of time."

The twins exchanged silent looks. Iana had done well. The villagers would not fear her now. If the sisters were careful about other skills, they would never have to worry about her being an outcast...or worse.

CHAPTER FIVE

Years slid by in a pattern as reliable as the seasons. Iana spent the day of every new moon in the village square, ready to answer questions. After the first rush, there were fewer who gathered, but she was never bored. It was one of the only times she played with other children her age. Her strangeness didn't bother them. She could not talk, but Batren couldn't hear and Shella had one leg shorter than the other. As long as she could keep up with them, she was welcome. She taught them ways to keep secrets and tricks for fooling their parents. She had ways of protecting them. Ways the children would never speak of. When Shella's brother tormented her one too many times, the children didn't ask how he fell from a perfectly mild-mannered horse so hard he broke his leg. They talked about the bone sticking through skin, and the way he screamed. But they never mentioned Iana.

The cabin became a place of visitors once again. Some questions were too delicate for the public new moon sessions and some couldn't wait. Iana would often invite the visitor to walk with her. She never ventured far from the cottage, but there was an air of privacy to the walks. As she grew in her role, she became better at answering questions with just her hands. Precious parchment could be saved for the nights when prophecy struck unsolicited.

One such night came when both twins were out. Iana was ten. Plenty old enough to be left on her own. The tinkers were in town and the villagers gathered in the square for music and drinking and dancing. Children were not permitted. It was autumn. The harvest had been brought in and stores set aside for the winter. Midiga and Sidanthe had joked about how busy life would become in the spring. Iana wasn't sure what they meant, but the husky laughter implied something for adults only.

And so, Iana was alone. She had already tended the garden. She had fixed her own dinner and cleaned up after herself. She was sitting by the fire, mending a cloak for Midiga as a surprise when the vision struck. The bone needle pierced her finger and she cried out, dropping cloak and thread. She fell to her knees, burning with the need to speak, but knowing that giving voice to her vision would silence her gift. Instead, she crawled to the carved chest and heaved it open, digging out charcoal and parchment. She hunched over her prize and scrawled across page after page.

When the frenzy passed, the candles had burned low. Iana was exhausted and wanted nothing more than to collapse in her bed. But a tingle warned her that this Seeing was for her alone. She gathered her pages and carefully rolled them into a tight cylinder. Instinct led her fingers to a weakness in stone by the fire. She hissed at the heat but managed to pry it up and tuck away her treasure. Tomorrow, while the sisters slept off the night's revelry, she would study her work. And learn.

***

Iana stood over Sidanthe as she slept. Midiga was out at a neighbour's, tending a birth. It had been a difficult pregnancy and she would likely be gone for the night. Since the incident with the fox, Iana had tested bodywalking on other animals. In the beginning, she limited herself to dead animals. She wasn't allowed to venture far, though, and few creatures were polite enough to drop dead at her feet. The first time she caught a rabbit and snapped its neck, she felt a thrill of power. She could control life *and* death. She learned to catch, kill, and hide the body. She knew instinctively that the twins would not approve of her activities, no matter her motivations.

It was pure frustration that taught her to inhabit a live animal. She had been watching the birds flying by. After running with wolves and climbing with squirrels, she wanted to fly. She had tried catching birds. Once, she succeeded and had held the trembling body, ready to break its neck with a sharp twist. The sparrow had been a heartbeat from death when Sidanthe's shadow fell across Iana's hands. She had turned and held the bird out proudly, keeping her expression carefully blank. Sidanthe pried her hands loose with a gentle admonition. After that, Iana was more determined than ever to experience flight. Over days, then weeks, she watched and watched and finally stomped a foot, growling her rage. On the heels of anger, or perhaps driven by it, success was hers. She had launched her soul into the small body. As if she was in the air with eyesight clearer than she could ever imagine. She felt the wind through her feathers. She saw a mouse racing through a field and restrained the urge to dive after it. Most thrilling of all, she could feel the eagle's heartbeat and the panic in the bird's mind. The soul fluttered and beat against her control. She tightened her grip and felt it cower. Such a magnificent creature, and it was hers to command.

Experiments followed: Sleeping animals; running animals; eating animals. She found that the more distracted a creature, the easier it was for her to slip in and gain control. Chipmunks and squirrels were the smoothest, but not very thrilling. The more intelligent, the more enjoyable its subjugation. She tested her range. How far could she stand from something and take over? She found that if she were very quiet and very still, she could see for miles. It took practice. She had never been beyond the village and didn't know where the world ended.

The twins watched her with pride, unaware that she wasn't meditating. They assumed she was turning inward to strengthen her seer talents, and she encouraged that belief. She began to make up prophecies to cover her activities. Simple, vague declarations that were easy to prove or dismiss. Seeing came all too easy, though. She could see the future of every life within her reach. The only life that wasn't clear was her own, but she was far too young to care. Seeing was dull. Control was addictive.

She looked upon Sidanthe and smiled. Her eyes slid closed, and she matched her breathing to Sidanthe's. Slow. Steady. She reached out, gently testing. There was a moment of surprise as she slipped easily into the sleeping woman's mind. Iana moved carefully. This mind was so much more than the others. Even the most intelligent creature was still fairly simple. Sidanthe was a huge maze spread out before her, with parts light and dark. Wide, inviting passages split off into narrow alleys. And the doors! So very many doors of every colour and shape. Some stood open. Some eased open as she passed. None of these caught her attention, though. It was a door ahead that she focused on. Wild vines grew over the surface, stretching across the walls and creeping to floor and ceiling. Everything about the door said:

"Keep out!" It was the only one Iana cared about. She considered the risk, once more testing and listening for the slightest indication that Sidanthe was aware of her. All remained quiet. Her smile deepened as she moved forward. She waved a hand, intending to sweep away the vines. Nothing happened. Iana frowned. Anyone watching Sidanthe's sleeping form would think she was dreaming as she, too, frowned.

Iana swept her hand again. Again, nothing. She moved closer. Waved a hand.

"Awww, nuts!"

Old habits die hard, but the words were not cute or child-like. They were laden with venom. Iana gave in to her rage and began tearing at the vines. Her scream of fury echoed through Sidanthe's mind and woke her in a state of terror.

Iana waited, coiled in the landscape of Sidanthe's mind, patient as a snake. She had expected the takeover of a sleeping soul to be easy. She was wrong. But she knew this woman knew her weaknesses and her pressure points. The battlefield may be unseen to a witness, but it was crystal clear to Iana.

For a long moment, Sidanthe struggled to grasp what was happening. Her head pounded, and the world seemed fuzzy and distant. She tried to sit up, but her body would not respond. She tried to speak, but no sound slipped free. The memory of a fox rubbing her leg surfaced, and she understood. Her voice turned inward.

"Iana, no! Stop!"

Her ward snarled as freshly torn vines reformed and clung stubbornly to the door. She wanted to know what was behind that wood. She would not be denied. Sidanthe reeled in pain and the battle for her mind began. She was unprepared for the raw onslaught that assaulted her meagre defences. She tried reacting as she would to a physical attack. Her arms attempted to reach out and drag Iana away from the door. When that had no effect, she tried to run and tackle the girl. That was when she realised that she could propel herself through her own mind. And while she could not touch Iana, she could reinforce her shields.

Iana growled as the surface of the door grew large, sharp thorns. Every time she reached for another vine to tear it away, her fingers were sliced open. Blood flowed from her hands and made her grip slippery. She stepped back and glared at Sidanthe. The edge of her lip curled, and her voice echoed down the halls, scattering to every shadowed corner of Sidanthe's mind.

"You would deny me? You who silenced me?

Who stole my heritage and refused to teach me properly? Had you bothered to truly know my mother; you would have expected all of this. I read your scrolls. I crafted my own. I know what you thought of her. Seer, are you? Blind, I say!"

Sidanthe coaxed the thorns, making them grow and push Iana back further. She could feel the walls all around them crumbling and knew that memories were dying. Perhaps skills. There was a strong chance that she would not live through this. For half a moment, the vines trembled and threatened to collapse as Sidanthe spared a thought of grief that it had all come to this. But she knew, instinctively, what lay behind that door. Her very soul pulsed, protected. Strong for now. If she died, her soul would join the spirits and either await rebirth or become a guardian. But if Iana got through, if that rage struck the core of her, there would be nothing left. There was no time to mourn or wonder. She couldn't spare the energy to understand. This was most certainly not a time for teaching. Her only hope was that they would both be capable of a conversation later. And with that final thought, she focused everything she was on the door as the walls continued to dissolve.

Iana ignored her bleeding hands. There was no pain, but as she lost more blood, she also lost energy. She was flagging. Her grip on more than just the vines weakened. Determination swelled and brought a fresh wave of madness. She stepped back from the door, sparing a glance at the wasteland around her. Sidanthe was on her knees, one hand stretched toward the door in desperation. The rest was darkness, spreading in all directions. The hallways and corridors had vanished, taking with them all the doors. All the memories. If Iana released her now, Sidanthe would be nothing more than a husk. But it wasn't in Iana to relent. She had a child's temper and a child's greed.

She smiled at the woman she had loved and learned from. And with a burst of strength that she had no control over, she ripped the walls off the last remaining room. The door stood, tangled in vine and thorn. But it no longer guarded a soul's haven. As the last stone turned to dust and blew away, Iana reached out and closed a bloody hand around the fluttering light that was Sidanthe. She heard a distant cry and power surged through her.

"Oh, Iana. What have you done?"

Iana slid back into her own body and stepped away from Sidanthe. She could feel the soul, throbbing gently. It was a part of her now. The power was hers. The memories held most secret and most dear. What Sidanthe could not speak aloud to another was Iana's for the taking.

A bird called out, and Iana looked to the door

of the cabin. Light was beginning to filter in. Daylight. Midiga would surely be home soon. Iana pulled the blanket over Sidanthe's still form. She sighed, fingers brushing the soft cheek. Sidanthe's eyes were wide open, but blank of life. Though she died in a rush of fear, she looked more sad than anything. Iana's knees began to buckle as the magnitude of her crime struck her. She had killed. She had stolen a soul. It was within her, not as a gift, but taken in violence. The child quivered and wanted to curl up against her adopted mother. A tear slid down her cheek. She tilted her head back and opened her throat to the wailing scream of grief. Her lips would not part and give form to the sound, but every creature within hearing distance ran or flew as fast as possible from the overwhelming emotion.

Midiga heard the cry as the far distant howl of a wolf and she paused on her journey back. She didn't fear wolves, but she was wise enough to be cautious. Something was driving her, though. Pushing her to be home. Something felt very wrong. She had been reaching for Sidanthe for hours and had found nothing where there had always been warmth. If the worst had happened and Sidanthe was dead, her spirit would be close by. Midiga had no doubt of that. So where was she? Why the cold? She hurried her steps, worried of what would come with the rising of the sun.

She slowed as she approached the cabin. She had not seen or heard a single woodland creature for the last hour. No birds sang in the morning, no insects protested the loss of night. Even the cat who slunk around in search of field mice was strangely absent. Midiga pushed the door open and blinked, letting her eyes adjust. There was Iana, sleeping by the hearth. The glow from the coals revealed the steady rise and fall of her chest. A smile pulled at Midiga. Such a sweet girl. Her gaze slid to Sidanthe in her narrow bed and agony gripped her heart, causing physical pain. She could no longer feel her sister. The body was there, but even from across the room, Midiga knew that it was an empty vessel. She swayed, reaching out for her twin's soul, for some shred of her other half. Since conception, she had been part of another. All the way home, she had pushed back the dread. Sidanthe had been studying bodywalking to better teach Iana how to control her talents. Midiga had told herself that her sister was safe and that the walking had somehow weakened their connection. It hadn't occurred to her—it never would—that Sidanthe had ceased to be entirely. Her gaze returned to the sleeping child. The coals crackled and glowed brighter briefly, and she saw the smile that tugged at sewn lips.

Midiga fled the cabin.

CHAPTER SIX

"Iana, please!"

"Iana. Iana. Iana no more. Sidanthe is here with me. She will always be with me." The girl's head tilted to the side. Her expression was far older than her years. Predatory. Considering. "We are one. You will call me Ianthe."

The voice rolled through her mind and Midiga shuddered in fear and revulsion. Souls could bind, but not like this. This was betrayal. This was depredation. Sidanthe was not a natural part of Iana. She was imprisoned. Possibly consumed. "No. No! You are not bound. You have devoured her. It is not our way, Iana. Please! Release her! Come back to us."

The child smiled, the expression gruesome. She looked towards the village and the air crackled with power. Her hands raised in the air. Lights quivered and danced as her fingers spread, then curled into fists. Once again, her voice rose, louder and full of rage.

"I....AM!"

A thousand meanings were wrapped in those two words, all of them resonating in every mind they struck. Rippling through the tiny town, declaring herself and making her strength known.

Villagers paused in their daily activities. At first, wonder filled them. They smiled and turned in Ianthe's direction. Though they could not see her, they knew her. She was their Seer. She had cared for them and given them hope, or at least truth, in some of their darkest personal moments. Now, they felt a love such as they had never known. They belonged. They were hers. Warmth suffused them and they fell to their knees. Just as they were bending their heads in supplication, her fury struck. Her smile deepened as every mind shattered under the force. All save one.

Midiga gripped her head, sobbing as the pain overwhelmed her senses. She rocked back and forth on her knees and tears splashed the dirt. Ianthe drank in the sight, savouring each detail. Midiga reached out with her own skills. She had always been able to account for all the villagers. She knew when a baby was born, or a man died. She knew when a child ventured too far from the huts. She even knew how many chickens and cows graced the farms.

They were all dead. Fayne and her daughter, named for Iana. Dask. Cydare was long gone, and Midiga spared a thought of gratitude that he hadn't witnessed this.

"Ia..." She paused. Her throat closed as her stomach threatened to kick back her last meal. The name was hard to force past her lips. "Ianthe. What have you done?"

"Declared myself. Taught them how to love. But also," She looked to the night sky, thinking. "But also ensured there would be no warnings. You won't tell anyone, will you, Midiga?"

That gaze turned and Midiga tried to sink into the ground. Her soul shrieked at her to run or hide or curl up and die. Stars whirled in Ianthe's eyes. Depthless. Fathomless. Colours swirled and Midiga understood the vastness of the universe. She who had never looked past her own village quivered under the knowledge. A whimper slipped from her and she could feel Ianthe's pleasure.

"No. You won't. You will worship me. You will love me. Yes." She spoke in her way, strolling the corridors of Midiga's thoughts. She seemed to talk to herself, mulling things over and setting her path. Restless, she moved. "This won't do. It won't do. No, not at all. It's all wrong. I need more. I need something... yes. That will do nicely."

Midiga closed her eyes to block out the rambling. The words were bad enough. They weren't her own, and the tone was painted with madness and a greed that went beyond anything material. She dared to look up and gasped, discovering a new horror. She would have turned and run had her legs not been made of water.

Ianthe held the pendant, staring at it with deep

interest. "You didn't know I found this, did you? You tried to hide it from me. It was my mother's, and you would have kept it from me."

She didn't sound angry, which was the only reason Midiga could still breathe. A dozen lies sprang to her lips, but laughter cut them all off. "I can read you, seer. Do not think to mislead me. You did not want me to have this. Why? What is that? The Twelve? What is The Twelve?"

Midiga put all her will in keeping that box closed. She tried to think of anything else. Cruel laughter became a visual thing in her mind's eye, dark pulsing clouds wrapping around the box of knowledge. Plucking at it.

"You would deny me? Sidanthe tried to deny me. She claimed she didn't know the purpose of the pendant. My mother. I can see her in your memories. You were scared of her, weren't you? She knew things. She would have taught me things.

Did you kill her? Did you?"

Midiga cringed back, "No! She died bringing you into the world. We could not save her."

"You didn't try very hard."

The seer remained silent. They hadn't tried, but only because they'd focused on saving the babe. There was truth in Ianthe's accusation. The twins had been afraid of Chani. There had always been such dark power in that one. In her youth, she had been sweet and kind. But she loved to explore and had come away from nearby caves with that infernal pendant. Midiga's eyes fell upon it again, and Ianthe's gaze narrowed.

"Sidanthe told me the truth. She didn't know the purpose. But you do, don't you? You read the old texts. Studied the old scrolls. You kept what you learned from her. You will not keep it from me!"

The box flew apart and Midiga cried out, once more clutching her head. She nearly passed out from that pain, but anguish and despair clung stubbornly to clarity.

Ianthe drew back in shock. She turned from the shaking oracle to the chain in her hand. "It can't be. All of that? In this? Truly?"

The voice in Midiga's mind carried the wonder of a twelve-year-old girl. She almost allowed herself to relax. It wasn't the same as hearing a person speak, when there were other things to compete with your attention, where you had the luxury of logic. This was all-encompassing. The sound of Ianthe's words blocked out everything.

Midiga could see the grass under her knees. She could hear the wind in the trees. She was aware of the total lack of bird calls. None of it mattered when Ianthe spoke. And now, when she spoke as a child, Midiga felt herself waver. She had been the first to hold her, had raised the girl as her own. The twins could never have children, but Ianthe had been theirs in everything but blood. She had taught the girl to walk and hunt. Sidanthe handled the more tender skills, but Midiga was responsible for teaching survival. Her heart softened. Surely it wasn't too late.

A hum filled the air. Midiga looked up to see Ianthe hold the pendant high. The voice had left her mind, granting a blessed but ominous silence. The wind picked up, swirling and angry. The hum grew louder. It was as if every bee that ever was had gathered in song.

All fell quiet.

The first to arrive were blue. There were four of them, perfect cubes with archaic symbols etched on all six sides. They spun on every axis and whirled around Ianthe, casting her in an eerie glowing light. Her laughter was childlike as it fluttered through Midiga. The humming returned with them, softer now. Ianthe reached to touch one, and it danced out of her way. She giggled again and clapped her hands.

The green came next, also four in number. Dread covered Midiga like a heavy blanket. The legends of old whispered to her. Ianthe was too consumed with delight, as the greens joined the blues, to notice the secret of The Twelve on the surface of Midiga's thoughts. It wouldn't matter, though. Soon, all would be revealed, and no one would be able to stop her. The humming grew louder and started to sound like chatter, as if they were speaking. Ianthe nodded. A smile formed and Midiga scooted back slightly.

With the arrival of the reds, the night took on an unearthly glow. The light from these drowned out the rest. The real power lay with them. The first four were a warning. The second a preparation. But the last were the slamming of a door.

The humming reached a crescendo, and the light swelled until it was near blinding.

Through the glow, Midiga could see Ianthe rise into the air, carried on shades of red, green, and blue. Her small body stretched and twisted, and every line of her silently screamed in agony. Midiga stood and took a step forward. A gust swept up and knocked her off her feet. She tried crawling to her ward, needing to save her. Ianthe had taken terrible, unforgivable actions, but she was a child. Surely, she wasn't lost. She could be taught and corrected. Midiga's fingers clawed at the dirt. She didn't realise she was screaming Iana's name until she tasted blood in the back of her throat.

The light grew incandescent and the sound louder. Both tangled into a bewildering cacophony. Then it stopped.

There wasn't a sound to be heard. Night had fallen, as dark as Iana's birthday. There was no moon. No stars shone. The breeze didn't even dare blow. It struck Midiga that it was mid-afternoon. She shook all over as she peered around, hoping to see some hint of light on the horizon. Could the entire world have been cast into darkness? What evil was this? What depth of power?

Slowly, the red glow returned. The artifacts still whirled, but they were far less frantic. They seemed to have expended all their energy and now spun lazy. Midiga tore her eyes from their dance to watch a slumped, naked figure unfold itself from the grass.

Ancient, tattered texts contained drawings of a demon goddess sent to punish the unwary. Some were crude, but a few artists were quite skilled at depicting the nightmare. Midiga watched as a work of terrifying art came to life. Nothing was left of the child Iana.

Ianthe paced back and forth, getting to know

this new form. She was taller, nearly twice her previous height. Her skin was pitch black, drinking in all light and throwing it back in the crimson beams that traced across her flesh. The patterns reminded Midiga of nights spent gazing up at the stars. Everyone knew they were the glow of spirits who had moved on from this world. To see blood-coloured stars pulsing just under the skin was a sacrilege. One in particular shone brighter than the rest, near Ianthe's heart, and Midiga knew its source. Her heart clenched as she whispered her sister's name.

Ianthe's burning gaze snapped to Midiga. Once more, she was overwhelmed with the vastness of what lay beyond her world. Where Iana had been born with leaf green eyes that echoed the forest, Ianthe's eyes were a blazing scarlet. Her voice changed as it hissed through Midiga's mind. Darker now. Older and tainted with too much knowledge.

"Sidanthe. Yes, the girl is still here. The sweet taste of struggle. She thinks to save me." Ianthe laughed and the sound turned Midiga's bowels to water.

Black hair tumbled from one side of her head, reaching nearly to the ground. The other side was completely bare. A multitude of horns grew in a crown, parting hair and straining skin. They curled high and over, turning to spirals as they slid down her back.

The newly reborn goddess held up one hand, turning it back and forth, examining the long stretches of claws curving into vicious points. Each looked as though it had been dipped in blood. She raised one to her lips and tapped at the stitching. Worn thread had been transformed into dark metal piercings. Midiga watched those claws and fought an overwhelming urge to crawl forward, begging to lick them. Her tongue slid over her lips with a sudden craving as the small primal side of herself screamed in abject terror.

Midiga dropped to her knees, unable to stand in such a presence, and averted her eyes from Ianthe's claret mouth. Her gaze fell on legs that belonged on a demon. Hooves larger than any horses' tore up grass as they carved a rut in the ground. Barbed horns sprung from bone and flesh, curving in all directions. Scales danced along goat legs, an extra knee bending the wrong way. They should have been ugly, and they were. They should have been frightening, and they were. Beyond measure. And yet. And yet.

Midiga's stare travelled up over sleek, powerful thighs that seemed to go on forever. A whip-like tail snapped back and forth behind long legs. It swept across the ground, burning grass where it touched. This creature was ancient when the concept of primordial was a babe. She was beyond words like evil and nefarious. She was born of the first pool of inky darkness. And yet. Midiga felt the craving intensify, blocking out every other sensation. She didn't care if it cost her immortal soul. She didn't care what the sacrifice. She needed to touch.

Laughter once again filled her mind and broke the spell. "Oh, no. I have need of you whole and clear. You are to be my Herald. No, don't whimper. You should be proud."

An icy wind swept through Midiga and she was once again herself. She scrambled to her feet and rubbed hands over her arms. So close. She had come so close to surrendering. She looked Ianthe over once more, testing. The hunger was still there, but it was a dull throb now, like a toothache that never reached past annoying. She could endure and resist. But she knew it would take very little to put her back on her knees, pleading.

CHAPTER SEVEN

Ianthe stood in a grove, with The Twelve reeling around her. She watched them, then waved her hand, scattering them. She breathed in deep. There was a frantic electricity when they were around. Power surged and rolled through her, pushing her to action. She still hadn't been able to sort out what that action was, but they made her restless. They spoke to her in buzzing whispers. When they were all together, they made no sense, chattering over each other like toddlers. But she found that if she summoned them by colour, they were less frenetic. Ianthe still couldn't understand them, but it became less about incoherent jabbering and more about language. There was a familiarity to their speech, but no recognition. She came to the grove alone, testing her theories. Ianthe had learned much in a short time.

She could invoke the blues alone, but not the greens without the blues. She could feel the greens, eager to join when she brought in the blues. But the reds were silent until she had the first eight and reached out for them. It was as if they needed an invitation.

The artifacts had abilities and personalities. She was playing with the blues one afternoon, for they were the most whimsical. They would zip in and out around her, performing an intricate ballet. It was when a rabbit ran too close that their true purpose was revealed. The rabbit squealed and writhed while Ianthe watched, fascinated. It jerked and stretched, body transforming from rabbit to fish. The feet, tail, and ears remained. The rest was a gasping mess that didn't last long. After that, Ianthe worked at controlling where and how the cubes moved. In time, she found that she could point them at a specific creature. What she couldn't dictate was what came after. But it was fun to try.

The blues altered when the greens came. It was as if they lost their ability to transform and simply whirled in mad patterns. But the greens had a talent all their own. They moulded the land and while they were quite content to wreak havoc and do as they wished, they also followed direction. Ianthe's private grove grew in size. It gained a stream and, a slope formed perfectly beneath her reclining shape. If the sun was too sharp, trees inevitably stretched out to offer shade, only to withdraw when the day cooled.

The reds were more difficult. Far more difficult.

She had worked with them over and over and was doing so yet again. Ianthe thought she had tasted power in the past. After all, she wiped out a village simply by willing it. She could walk through any mind, take over any body. But when she tapped into the red artifacts, she felt more…endless possibilities. The galaxies she had glimpsed during her metamorphosis, the ones that whirled in her eyes, were opened to her. It was all too easy to get lost in those journeys. She could gaze upon the vastness and wonder or lean in on a planet and see its people in their daily lives. But under the surface, she knew there was more to the reds. She was missing something vital, and they were not giving up their secrets easily.

She was sure, if she could unlock the full Twelve, she would have access to the most cardinal of elements. The first from which all others sprung.

Ianthe leaned back against her slope, watching the swirling artifacts. The first eight kept their distance unless she summoned them forward. It was as if they were frightened of the reds. At the very least, they seemed subservient. They had been eager to show her what they could do for her, but now gave up the stage. She had taken to thinking of the reds as the Imperial ones. Regal and cool for all their fiery colour. She couldn't decide if they were being coy, hoping she would tease their secret out or if they simply didn't care. Her hand lifted as she traced a pattern. Infinity looping through the air. She focused her eye on her finger, doing her best to ignore the cubes. It would be too easy to let the others distract her. They were so much fun. This was work. Important work.

An hour passed. Then two. She continued to draw the pattern. Even though she hadn't got so much as a twitch from the reds, she felt it was the right thing to do. Her arm was growing weary and her vision wanted to blur. Her mind kept trying to wander. The edges of her vision rippled with stars, and she wanted nothing more than to lay back and explore them. Boredom rode temptation like a trained pony. She could simply canter off and lose the afternoon to far-flung glory.

She growled and shook her head, eyesight never faltering from that single claw. Another hour. As the fourth arrived, she was granted a clue. The blues, which had been playing out a pirouette all day, suddenly stopped. They settled into the grass and quieted. Their light reduced to a gentle throb. Ianthe nearly lost her pattern, fumbling it a little.

She took a deep breath and steadied herself. She considered calling out for Midiga to bring her sustenance, but that same knowing arose. This was a private ceremony, and if she failed this chance, there would not be another. She pushed down the hunger and thirst, tucking them away into a place that did not matter and would not distract.

Her finger moved in a steady motion.

On the eighth hour, when the sun was resting, and the night grew cool, the greens joined the blues in their slumber. Now the grove was lit ruby, with undertones of sapphire and emerald. The reds hovered. They had not yet moved from their original spot, but Ianthe could sense a building in them; a gathering of energy and intent. Again, she knew. Where the others had gleefully given themselves to her, this would be a battle. She had to earn whatever the reds could offer. If she wasn't found worthy, she would likely be found dead. And yet, there was no hesitation in her. She didn't for a moment consider the risk and the cost. All through her childhood, she heard Sidanthe and Midiga speak of Destiny. It was always a big word for the small Iana to take in. Destiny. It drove you and decided you. She grew believing it was her Destiny to be Seer to her tribe. What small thinkers her mothers had been.

She wanted to stroke Sidanthe. There was always a little thrill when she touched that pure soul. She took pleasure in the fear that never left her mother. She thrilled at the unending despair. But most of all, she was fascinated by the continual pulse of hope. Sidanthe knew her body was gone. She knew she was trapped. She knew she had no power. And still she hoped. If she had given in to desperation, Ianthe might have grown weary and consumed her entirely. But this tendril of hope, this small island upon which Sidanthe huddled, was a spice unlike any she'd tasted.

Ianthe didn't reach out. She shook her head again to clear the distraction. Hour nine approached.

As the tenth crested, Ianthe heard her father. He called out to her as he strode toward her grove. Her head tilted slightly, eyes narrowing, finger never stilling. This could not be. Her father died with the rest of his tribe. This creature descending on her with anger flashing was an illusion. An agitation. A diversion. It almost worked. Just as she had plucked the truth of her mother from Sidanthe's thoughts, so had she learned of her father. But where she was fascinated by her mother, her father was nothing to her. So why was her heart fluttering and her belly tightening to see him bearing down on her? He swept past the artifacts and loomed, glaring.

"What are you playing at, child? This is forbidden!"

Her body tensed, ready to stand and face him. Her throat clenched in preparation of response. Her finger wobbled.

"No," she murmured softly and looked past him. The reds had paused in their rotations. All four hung in the air. The hour passed and her father, still raging and berating, faded from her sight.

Relief nearly overwhelmed her. Through her weariness, she understood. This battle was more than just endurance. It was more than mere interference. She was being tested for not just her strengths, but her weaknesses. There was no doubt in her mind that any vulnerability shown would be noted and used against her, whether she won or lost.

Her finger traced the pattern. Over and over.

Her eyes grew tired. Eyelashes are light, airy things, but hers felt like boulders. They pulled at her lids, dragging them downward and threatening to block out the once more spinning cubes. Her hand sagged but kept moving. The night was heavy around her, but not unpleasant. It was a blanket, tucked in to keep out a chill. It was a warm kiss on the forehead. It was comfort and safety and a promise. It was love.

Ianthe blinked savagely, her gaze never breaking for more than the slightest whisper of a moment. She cursed so loud and long that Midiga, far away at their encampment, snapped awake in terror. The seer would spend the rest of the night huddled by a fire, frantically watching the darkness. Ianthe gained control and broke the connection. She even laughed a little and bent her head slightly with respect. "Oh, well done. But you will not have me yet."

The eleventh hour passed.

A mist rose slow to cover the land, growing thicker as it crept closer. Ianthe saw it from the edges of her vision. It swept over the grass, but also over the stars in her mind's eye. Both began to wither. Grass curled over and turned brown, clear even in the dark of the night. Stars flickered and gasped, then faded. This mist was Death. Just as Ianthe knew Destiny was a force, so she knew this was not mere death. This was Death. And it was coming for her.

She tried to brace herself. The pain of her transformation had been all consuming. Surely nothing the mist brought could be any worse than a body being torn apart and reformed. She redoubled her focus on the infinity pattern and did her best to ignore the white cloud.

Tendrils lifted and stretched. Where they touched trees, bark turned to ash. When they wrapped around blue and green cubes, light died. When they reached Ianthe, she knew true fear.

The strands of fog hovered over her skin and swayed before her finger. They had not yet touched her, but she knew it wouldn't be long. Ianthe wasn't fond of fear. It was a useful tool with which to control others, but it served no purpose on a personal level. Fear was supposed to keep you from harm. It was supposed to warn of impending doom and give you a chance to avoid damage. None of that concerned her. Fear was useless and distracting. But while she could ignore Sidanthe, banish a vision and ignore bone-deep fatigue, she couldn't get past this.

The tendrils moved in a hypnotic fashion and she found her finger moving in time with them. Still drawing the same pattern, but only by sheer force of will. She had once watched a snake sway to lull its dinner. The prey had begun to move with the snake and a heartbeat later, it was dead. Ianthe held on to that lesson as the dread built.

Without warning, her world shattered. The Twelve gathered and clashed together, banishing the dark in an explosion of colour. The loudest of thunderclaps split the air. The fog struck and

Ianthe's pattern finally ceased, at the exact moment the twelfth hour fell.

She arched and screamed as the mist enveloped her and dipped her body in liquid fire. Her flesh refused to burn away. Nerve endings clung stubbornly to their task. Had she actually been set alight, she would at least have the comfort of an imminent end. Ianthe wasn't that lucky. Instead, she twisted on the ground and cried out her agony, clawing at the grass. Her body blazed in a flameless inferno and her mind broke.

She sat in the embrace of the largest tree she had ever seen. Her entire tribe, joined hand to hand, could not encircle its span. She looked up, seeing nothing but limbs; branches stretching into eternity. Looking down made her dizzy as the bark fell away into stars and mist.

The mist.

Ianthe had clambered out of it. She watched it

reach and grasp, fog becoming long menacing fingers. She huddled closer to the tree and laid her cheek against its strength. All the fight left her in a rush. Tears coursed down her cheeks.

This was it, was it? Was this where she would end? Had she failed the test? All that power and all that promise. Lost to her now. She stretched out a questioning tendril of her own towards Midiga. Nothing. Panic stirred and she turned inward for Sidanthe. Sidanthe, who could never leave her. Nothing. Silence. She was alone. Tears clogged in her throat, threatening to choke her. Since her birth, Ianthe had never been alone. Even when experimenting with her talents, she could feel the twins nearby. Despondent, she looked around for someone. For anyone. For the smallest hint of life.

At the end of her branch, a dark flower unfurled. She'd never seen anything like it. Long petals peeled back and unrolled, then tucked under, revealing deep shades of blue. Another layer of petal, shorter than the first, stretched lazy, the edges kissed purple. At the very centre, silver stamen rippled in an unfelt breeze. Ianthe crawled toward the flower, wrapping arms and legs around the branch. She paused where the limb grew thin and strained her fingers. She had to touch the flower. She had to.

A thorn bit deep into her finger, stopping her cold with a burst of fresh pain. Ianthe pulled back her hand and watched as blood welled up. After the agony of the fire, after the torment of the fog, she could feel something as mundane as a thorn prick. Underscoring the sharp bite came another sensation. One she had nearly forgotten. Pleasure shivered over her skin, warming her loins. Lately, her only pleasure had been taken at the cost of another. Ianthe had watched and relished. But this was all hers and, small though it may be, it was glorious.

She reached out again for that same thorn and offered it another finger. Her body jolted as her flesh was punctured again. A smile formed on her lips. She tilted her hand and stared at a droplet of blood as it fell to the mists below.

One tendril of Death stretched, hungry for the crimson sacrifice. A mouth formed, ragged with ethereal fangs. The droplet landed, and the fog shuddered. Fear licked at Ianthe, but the mist shook again. It shifted colours, from white to grey to mud. From the centre, a glow formed. Prismatic shards cut through the mud. In moments, the cloud lost its menace and Ianthe knew this was her way home. On impulse, she hugged the branch, sending a thought of gratitude.

And then she let go and tumbled into the kaleidoscope.

Ianthe sat up, gasping. She was back in her grove. Dawn was breaking and a light wind washed over still-hot flesh. She stood and held out a hand. The Twelve rushed to her, spinning in a flurry.

Ianthe focused on the blues. With a snap of her hand, they darted off to cast their glow around a chipmunk. She smiled as tiny squeals reached her ears. She laughed as an equally tiny wolfmunk ran into a hole in the ground. She turned to the greens and flicked her wrist. Her stream widened and water rushed to fill in the space, becoming a surging river.

With respect and care, Ianthe looked up to the reds. She understood now. Where she could demand and cajole from the others, she must ask of the reds. They were raw power and if she could not control them, they would spend eternity devouring her. She bowed low, hands folded in front of her. When she rose, the artifacts rejoined. They formed an arch, spinning faster until they were no more than a blur.

Within the confines of the arch, Ianthe could see a path. At the end of the path, Midiga prepared her morning meal. The chatter began anew, and she realised how silent they had all been through her trials. But she could distinguish voices now. The higher, lighter tones of the blues. The rumbles of the greens. The menacing whispers that could only be the reds. And she knew what they were saying. It wasn't so much an understanding as it was suddenly having the information she needed. She nodded and bowed again, closing the portal.

Ianthe looked toward the rising sun and smiled, savouring the tug of the piercings. She was complete. She had come into her full power.

Let the Universe tremble.

ABOUT THE AUTHOR

Kimberly Rei does her best work in the places that can't exist...the in-between places where imagination defies reality.

With a penchant for creepy shadows and hooks that leave you guessing, she can be found in anthologies from Black Hare Press, Eerie River Publishing, and Iron Faerie Publishing as well as behind the scenes of various collections editing, beta reading, marketing, and encouraging fellow authors.

Bibliography:

ANCIENTS, Black Hare Press, 2020

APOCALYPSE, Black Hare Press, 2019

Darkness Reclaimed, Eerie River Publishing, 2020

Forgotten Ones, Eerie River Publishing, 2020

HATE, Black Hare Press, 2020

It Calls From the Forest, Volume 2, Eerie River Publishing, 2020

LOVE, Black Hare Press, 2020

OCEANS, Black Hare Press, 2020

Quietus 13, Black Hare Press, 2020

The Best of Iron Faerie Publishing 2019, Iron Faerie Publishing, 2020

Connect:

Website: Tales.studiorei.org

Amazon: amazon.com/Askani-Aichi/e/B012LXAZV2

Twitter: @seersdaughter

Facebook: @reitales

ABOUT THE PUBLISHER

BLACK HARE PRESS is a small, independent publisher based in Melbourne, Australia.

Founded in 2018, our aim has always been to champion emerging authors from all around the globe and offer opportunities for them to participate in speculative fiction and horror short story anthologies.

Connect

Website: *www.blackharepress.com*

Twitter: *@BlackHarePress*